Wordspells

by the same author

MAGIC MIRROR
And other poems for children

MIDNIGHT FOREST
And other poems

WORD-SPELLS

chosen by
Judith Nicholls

illustrated by
Alan Baker

faber and faber
LONDON · BOSTON

First published in 1988
by Faber and Faber Limited
3 Queen Square London WC1N 3AU

Photoset by Parker Typesetting Service Leicester
Printed in Great Britain by
Mackays of Chatham Ltd

British Library Cataloguing in Publication Data

Wordspells
I. Nicholls, Judith
821'.914'0809282   PZ8.3
ISBN 0-571-14891-3

For my parents,
with love

Contents

In the text, the dates of those authors who died before 1900 are given at their first appearance in this anthology.

Introduction

Compiling an anthology begins as an indulgence but quickly turns into a sorry realization that including everything one would like to share will be quite impossible! Some favourites must be left out because of difficulties of thought or language for younger readers, others because as the collection developed there was no suitable place to present them to their best advantage, many because of lack of space.

No anthology can do justice either to poetry as a whole or to any individual poet. On the other hand few young people are going to buy the eighty or more individual volumes which would be needed merely to cover the writers included here. In a compiler's ideal world an anthology is in part a starting point which will send its readers full-pace to search out more of particular poets. In reality, this will not always happen, and it must aim at being sufficiently balanced to stand alone.

Most readers will, I hope, find something here which particularly appeals to them. There are poems to celebrate, to disturb and to amuse; poems which echo like music in our subconscious before they are really understood; poems which say in just three or four lines what would take pages of prose to explain. There are poems which seem to eliminate distances of time or place, linking us in celebration with an early Ireland or nineteenth century America, with Africa or the land of Solomon; in sorrow with a Chinese emperor writing two thousand years ago.

The best poetry sings and it illuminates. When it sings, like Philip Larkin's *The North Ship* or Ted Hughes's *The Warm and The Cold*, it doesn't matter if it is not wholly 'understood'. It will repay many readings, and with each one a little more of the music will be revealed for us – and the illumination. *'Le poète est celui qui regarde,'* said Gide; the poet is he who *looks*. The best poems are those which help us to look, and to see and feel more clearly than we might otherwise have done. Here, I hope, is a taste of just a few of them.

Judith Nicholls
February 1987

Counting-out Rhyme

Silver bark of beech, and sallow
Bark of yellow birch and yellow
　　Twig of willow.

Stripe of green in moosewood maple,
Colour seen in leaf of apple,
　　Bark of popple.

Wood of popple pale as moonbeam,
Wood of oak for yoke and barn-beam,
　　Wood of hornbeam.

Silver bark of beech, and hollow
Stem of elder, tall and yellow
　　Twig of willow.

Edna St Vincent Millay

1

Did You Ever, Ever, Ever?

Did you ever, ever, ever,
In your leaf, life, loaf,
See the deevel, divil, dovol,
Kiss his weef, wife, woaf?
No, I never, never, never,
In my leaf, life, loaf,
Saw the deevel, divil, dovol,
Kiss his weef, wife, woaf.

Traditional

Marigold Pie

'Say what you will,
You won't pass by
If you can't make a
Marigold pie.'

'Let me pass!
I don't lie
And I can make a
Marigold pie.

'Marigold petals.
Two small stones,
Lawn-grass clippings,
Chicken bones,
A spider's web with one dead fly
All mixed up in the wink of an eye.
And here it is for you to try.'

'Thanks, but no thanks – pass on by.'

Dennis Doyle

The Hangman's Tree

'Hangman, hangman, hold your hand,
   O hold it just a while!
For there I see my father coming,
   Riding many a mile.

'Father, have you brought me gold?
   Will you set me free?
Or have you come to see me hung
   From the hangman's tree?'

'No, I haven't brought you gold,
   I will not set you free,
But I have come to see you hung
   From the hangman's tree.'

'Hangman, hangman, hold your hand,
   O hold it just a while!
For there I see my mother coming,
   Riding many a mile.

'Mother, have you brought me gold?
   Will you set me free?
Or have you come to see me hung
   From the hangman's tree?'

'No, I haven't brought you gold,
   I will not set you free,
But I have come to see you hung
   From the hangman's tree.'

'Hangman, hangman, hold your hand,
    O hold it just a while!
For there I see my sister coming,
    Riding many a mile.

'Sister, have you brought me gold?
    Will you set me free?
Or have you come to see me hung
    From the hangman's tree?'

'No, I haven't brought you gold,
    I will not set you free,
But I have come to see you hung
    From the hangman's tree.'

'Hangman, hangman, hold your hand,
    O hold it just a while!
For there I see my sweetheart coming,
    Riding many a mile.

'Sweetheart, have you brought me gold?
    Will you set me free?
Or have you come to see me hung
    From the hangman's tree?'

'Yes, O yes, I've brought you gold,
    I will set you free,
For I have come to take you down
    From the hangman's tree.'

Traditional

The Gardener

The gardener stood at the garden gate,
    A primrose in his hand;
He saw a lovely girl come by,
    Slim as a willow wand.

'O lady, can you fancy me,
    And will you share my life?
All my garden flowers are yours,
    If you will be my wife.

'The white lily will be your shirt
    It suits your body best;
With cornflowers in your hair,
    A red rose on your breast.

'Your gloves will be the marigold,
    Glittering on your hand;
Your dress will be the sweet-william
    That grows upon the bank.'

'Young man, I cannot be your wife;
    I fear it will not do.
Although you care for me,' she said,
    'I cannot care for you.

'As you've provided clothes for me
    Among the summer flowers,
So I'll provide some clothes for you
    Among the winter showers.

'The fallen snow will be your shirt,
    It suits your body best;
Your head will be wound with the eastern wind,
    With the cold rain on your breast.

'Your boots will be of the seaweed
    That drifts upon the tide;
Your horse will be the white wave –
    Leap on, young man, and ride!'

Traditional

Fortunes

One for sorrow, two for joy,
Three for a kiss and four for a boy,
Five for silver, six for gold,
Seven for a secret never to be told,
Eight for a letter from over the sea,
Nine for a lover as true as can be.

Traditional

Miller's End

When we moved to Miller's End,
   Every afternoon at four
A thin shadow of a shade
   Quavered through the garden-door.

Dressed in black from top to toe
   And a veil about her head
To us all it seemed as though
   She came walking from the dead.

With a basket on her arm
   Through the hedge-gap she would pass,
Never a mark that we could spy
   On the flagstones or the grass.

When we told the garden-boy
   How we saw the phantom glide,
With a grin his face was bright
   As the pool he stood beside.

'That's no ghost-walk,' Billy said,
   'Nor a ghost you fear to stop –
Only old Miss Wickerby
   On a short cut to the shop.'

So next day we lay in wait,
   Passed a civil time of day,
Said how pleased we were she came
   Daily down our garden-way.

Suddenly her cheek it paled,
  Turned, as quick, from ice to flame.
'Tell me,' said Miss Wickerby.
  'Who spoke of me, and my name?'

'Bill the garden-boy.'
                        She sighed,
Said, 'Of course, you could not know
How he drowned – that very pool –
A frozen winter – long ago.'

Charles Causley

I Know Things

I know things at the side of my head
Like how to fetch the summer home
And how the sands move,
How lustre wanders in mirrors.
But I'm not telling.

I see things at the back of my head
Like where the conversations go
And frosted breath lives,
Where winds gather before they roam.
But I'm not telling. Not ever.

I hear things at the top of my head
Like what sheet music whispers
And what the leaves want,
What letters say before they're a word.
But I'm not telling. Not ever.

Only if you ask!

Adèle Davide

The Painter

She has a hidden eye
behind her eyes
that sees in drab brown fields
    lush, purple pie-crust corduroy; a river
    swishing as a tiger's tail of pink and gold.

A rook hops, bops and
meddles through its
private rooky day –
    she fixes him. A brooding shadow casts
    an eerie chill across the middle ground.

For storm grey skies
she captures
    livid greens blood reds and
    fearful nightmare blacks;
I look and shudder
    somewhere deep inside
    a frightened creature wakes.

Her paintings speak in shapes and colours
I can never see, but know are true:
I try to paint the things I see
    but she can see the things she paints –
    she has the gift, the second sight
    to make things new.

Mick Gowar

What My Lady Did

I asked my lady what she did
   She gave me a silver flute and smiled.
A musician I guessed, yes that would explain
   Her temperament so wild.

I asked my lady what she did
   She gave me a comb inlaid with pearl.
A hairdresser I guessed, yes that would explain
   Each soft and billowing curl.

I asked my lady what she did
   She gave me a skein of wool and left.
A weaver I guessed, yes that would explain
   Her fingers long and deft.

I asked my lady what she did
   She gave me a slipper trimmed with lace.
A dancer I guessed, yes that would explain
   Her suppleness and grace.

I asked my lady what she did
   She gave me a picture not yet dry.
A painter I guessed, yes that would explain
   The steadiness of her eye.

I asked my lady what she did
   She gave me a fountain pen of gold.
A poet I guessed, yes that would explain
   The strange stories that she told.

I asked my lady what she did
　　She told me – and oh, the grief!
I should have guessed, she's under arrest
　　My lady was a thief!

Roger McGough

Nose, Nose, Jolly Red Nose

Nose, nose, jolly red nose,
And who gave thee this jolly red nose?
Nutmegs and ginger, cinnamon and cloves,
And they gave me this jolly red nose.

Francis Beaumont (1584–1616)
and *John Fletcher* (1579–1625)

My Papa's Waltz

The whiskey on your breath
Could make a small boy dizzy;
But I hung on like death:
Such waltzing was not easy.

We romped until the pans
Slid from the kitchen shelf;
My mother's countenance
Could not unfrown itself.

14

The hand that held my wrist
Was battered on one knuckle;
At every step you missed
My right ear scraped a buckle.

You beat time on my head
With a palm caked hard by dirt,
Then waltzed me off to bed
Still clinging to your shirt.

Theodore Roethke

What Are Heavy?

What are heavy? Sea-sand and sorrow;
What are brief? Today and tomorrow;
What are frail? Spring blossoms and youth;
What are deep? The ocean and truth.

Christina Rossetti
(1830–94)

15

Grim and Gloomy

Oh, grim and gloomy
So grim and gloomy
Are the caves beneath the sea.
Oh, rare but roomy
And bare and boomy,
Those salt sea caverns be.

Oh, slim and slimy
Or grey and grimy
Are the animals of the sea.
Salt and oozy
And safe and snoozy
The caves where those animals be.

Hark to the shuffling,
Huge and snuffling,
Ravenous, cavernous,
great sea-beasts!
But fair and fabulous,
Tintinnabulous,
Gay and fabulous are their feasts.

Ah, but the queen of the sea,
The querulous, perilous sea!
How the curls of her tresses
The pearls on her dresses,
Sway and swirl in the waves,
How cosy and dozy,
How sweet ring-a-rosy
Her bower in the deep-sea caves.

Oh, rare but roomy
And bare and boomy
Those caverns under the sea,
And grave and grandiose,
Safe and sandiose
The dens of her denizens be.

James Reeves

The Waves of the Sea

Don't you go too near the sea,
  The sea is sure to wet you.
Harmless though she seems to be
  The sea's ninth wave will get you!
But I can see the small white waves
  That want to play with me –
They won't do more than wet my feet
  When I go near the sea.

Don't you go too near the sea,
  She does not love a stranger.
Eight untroubled waves has she,
  The ninth is full of danger!
But I can see the smooth blue waves
  That want to play with me –
They won't do more than wet my knees
  When I go near the sea.

17

Don't you go too near the sea,
  She'll set her waves upon you.
Eight will treat you playfully,
  Until the ninth has won you.
But I can see the big green waves
  That want to play with me –
They won't do more than wet my waist
  When I go near the sea.

Don't you go too near the sea,
  Her ways are full of wonder.
Her first eight waves will leave you free,
  Her ninth will take you under!
But I can see the great grey waves
  That want to play with me –
They won't do more than wet my neck
  When I go near the sea.

Don't you go too near the sea –
   O Child, you set me quaking!
Eight have passed you silently,
   And now the ninth is breaking!
I see a wave as high as a wall
   That wants to play with me –
O Mother, O Mother, it's taken me all,
   For I went too near the sea!

Eleanor Farjeon

Winter Ocean

Many-maned scud-thumper, tub
of male whales, maker of worn wood, shrub-
ruster, sky-mocker, rave!
portly pusher of waves, wind-slave.

John Updike

The Viking Terror

There's a wicked wind tonight,
Wild upheaval in the sea;
No fear now that the Viking hordes
Will terrify me.

Anon, about AD 800
(translated from Irish by Brendan Kennelly)

20

Low-Tide

These wet rocks where the tide has been,
  Barnacled white and weeded brown
And slimed beneath to a beautiful green,
  These wet rocks where the tide went down
Will show again when the tide is high
  Faint and perilous, far from shore,
No place to dream, but a place to die:
  The bottom of the sea once more.

There was a child that wandered through
  A giant's empty house all day, –
House full of wonderful things and new,
  But no fit place for a child to play!

                    Edna St Vincent Millay

Tell Me, Tell Me, Sarah Jane

Tell me, tell me, Sarah Jane,
    Tell me, dearest daughter,
Why are you holding in your hand
    A thimbleful of water?
Why do you hold it to your eye
    And gaze both late and soon
From early morning light until
    The rising of the moon?

Mother, I hear the mermaids cry,
    I hear the mermen sing,
And I can see the sailing-ships
    All made of sticks and string.
And I can see the jumping fish,
    The whales that fall and rise
And swim about the waterspout
    That swarms up to the skies.

Tell me, tell me, Sarah Jane,
    Tell your darling mother,
Why do you walk beside the tide
    As though you loved none other?
Why do you listen to a shell
    And watch the billows curl,
And throw away your diamond ring
    And wear instead the pearl?

Mother, I hear the water
  Beneath the headland pinned,
And I can see the seagull
  Sliding down the wind.
I taste the salt upon my tongue
  As sweet as sweet can be.

Tell me, my dear, whose voice you hear?

  It is the sea, the sea.

Charles Causley

Full Fathom Five

Full fathom five thy father lies,
  Of his bones are coral made;
Those are pearls that were his eyes;
  Nothing of him that doth fade,
But doth suffer a sea-change
Into something rich and strange.
Sea-nymphs hourly ring his knell:
  Ding-dong.
Hark! now I hear them – Ding-dong bell.

William Shakespeare (1564–1616)

Seal Lullaby

Oh! hush thee, my baby, the night is behind us,
And black are the waters that sparkled so green.
The moon, o'er the combers, looks downward to find us
At rest in the hollows that rustle between.
Where billow meets billow, there soft be thy pillow;
Ah, weary wee flipperling, curl at thy ease!
The storm shall not wake thee, nor sharks overtake thee,
Asleep in the arms of the slow-swinging seas.

Rudyard Kipling

Sea Timeless Song

Hurricane come
and hurricane go
but sea . . . sea timeless
sea timeless
sea timeless
sea timeless
sea timeless.

Hibiscus bloom
then dry-wither so
but sea . . . sea timeless
sea timeless
sea timeless
sea timeless
sea timeless.

Tourist come
and tourist go
but sea . . . sea timeless
sea timeless
sea timeless
sea timeless
sea timeless.

Grace Nichols

The Whales off Wales

With walloping tails, the whales off Wales
Whack waves to wicked whitecaps.
And while they snore on their watery floor,
They wear wet woollen nightcaps.

The whales! the whales! the whales off Wales,
They're always spouting fountains.
And as they glide through the tilting tide,
They move like melting mountains.

X. J. Kennedy

About the Teeth of Sharks

The thing about a shark is – teeth,
One row above, one row beneath.

Now take a close look. Do you find
It has another row behind?

Still closer – here, I'll hold your hat:
Has it a third row behind that?

Now look in and . . . Look out! Oh my,
I'll *never* know now! Well, goodbye.

John Ciardi

Yellow Butter

Yellow butter purple jelly red jam black bread
Spread it thick
Say it quick
Yellow butter purple jelly red jam black bread
Spread it thicker
Say it quicker
Yellow butter purple jelly red jam black bread
Now repeat it
While you eat it
Yellow butter purple jelly red jam black bread
Don't talk with your mouth full!

Mary Ann Hoberman

Peas

I eat my peas with honey,
I've done it all my life;
It makes the peas taste funny,
But it keeps them on the knife.

Anon

29

Whole Duty of Children

A child should always say what's true
And speak when he is spoken to,
And behave mannerly at table;
At least as far as he is able.

Robert Louis Stevenson (1850–94)

To Make a Prairie

To make a prairie it takes a clover
    and one bee,
One clover, and a bee,
And revery.
The revery alone will do,
If bees are few.

Emily Dickinson (1830–86)

Bee

You want to make some honey?
All right. Here's the recipe.
Pour the juice of a thousand flowers
Through the sweet tooth of a Bee.

X. J. Kennedy

31

The Flower-Fed Buffaloes

The flower-fed buffaloes of the spring
In the days of long ago,
Ranged where the locomotives sing
And the prairie flowers lie low:–
The tossing, blooming, perfumed grass
Is swept away by the wheat,
Wheels and wheels and wheels spin by
In the spring that still is sweet.
But the flower-fed buffaloes of the spring
Left us, long ago.
They gore no more, they bellow no more,
They trundle around the hills no more:–
With the Blackfeet, lying low,
With the Pawnees, lying low,
Lying low.

Vachel Lindsay

Leopard

Gentle hunter
his tail plays on the ground
while he crushes the skull.

Beautiful death
who puts on a spotted robe
when he goes to his victim.

Playful killer
whose loving embrace
splits the antelope's heart.

Yoruba Poem

The Cowboy's Lament

Oh, bury me not on the lone prairie,
Where the wild kiyotes will howl o'er me;
Where the rattlesnakes hiss and the wind blows free,
Oh, bury me not on the lone prairie!

They heeded not his dying prayer,
They buried him there on the lone prairie,
In a little box just six by three,
His bones now rot on the lone prairie.

American Traditional

Song of the Fishing Ghosts

Night is the time when phantoms play,
   Flows the river,
   Phantoms white
   Phantoms black
Fish in the dark salt water bay.

Skulls are nets for phantom fishers,
   Flows the river,
Phantoms red on a phantom river
   Dark flows the river.

Black phantom splashes
  Flows the river,
White phantom splashes
  Flows the river.

Night is the time when phantoms play,
  Heads are nets
  For phantom fishers
There on the dark salt water bay.

  Phantoms black
  Phantoms red
  Phantoms white
  For nets their heads
And the dark, dark, dark river flows.

Efua Sutherland

He who would seek her in the clear stream,
Let him go softly, as in a dream,
He who would hold her well,
Let him first whisper the spell
Of her names.

The silver one, the shimmering maiden,
The milkwhite-throated bride,
The treasure-bringer from the sea,
Leaper of weirs, hurdler to the hills,
The returning native, egg-carrier,
The buxom lass, the wary one,
The filly that shies from a moving shadow,
The darter-away, the restless shiner,
Lurker in alder roots,
The fearful maid.

Night dancer, ring maker,
The one that splinters reflections,
The splasher, the jester, the teaser, the mocker,
The false encourager, tweaker of lures,
The girl who is fasting, destroyer of hopes,
Bender of steel, the breaker, the smasher,
The strong wench, the cartwheeler,
The curve of the world,
She who doesn't want to surrender,
The desired, the sweet one.

When you've spent nights and days
Speaking her names, learning her ways,
Take down your tackle from the shelf,
And your skill. She may give herself
For the whispered spell.

Tom Rawling

The Angler's Lament

Sometimes over early,
Sometimes over late,
Sometimes no water,
Sometimes a spate,
Sometimes over thick,
And sometimes over clear.
There's aye something wrong
When I'm fishing here.

Anon

Water

The ice-cap slowly melts and drips,
   Tall icebergs float among tall ships.
From arctic wastes the waters flow,
   To make the seas and oceans grow.

Tempests and tides and roaring waves,
   Have carved out arches, cliffs and caves,
Water creates and shapes the land,
   From mountain range to grain of sand.

Up through the rivers water reaches,
   Past headlands, deltas, cliffs and beaches.
From the rivers, little streams,
   Spread through the land in glints and gleams.

The water-tank, up in the loft,
   A liquid cube, pure, cold and soft,
Waits to rush out from tap to air,
   And link you with the polar bear.

Leo Carey (aged 12)

The Dragonfly

There was once a terrible monster
lived in a pond, deep under the water.

Brown as mud he was, in the mud he hid,
among murk of reed-roots, sodden twigs,
with his long hungry belly,
six legs for creeping,
eyes like headlights
awake or sleeping;
but he was not big.

A tiddler came to sneer and jeer
and flaunt his flashing tail –
Ugly old stick-in-the-mud
couldn't catch a snail!
I'm not scared –
when, like a shot,
two pincers nab him, and he's got!

For the monster's jaw hides a clawed stalk
like the arm of a robot, a dinner fork,
that's tucked away cunningly till the last minute –
shoots out – and back with a victim in it!

Days, weeks, months, two years and beyond,
fear of the monster beset the pond;
he lurked, grabbed, grappled, gobbled and grew,
ambushing always somewhere new –

Who saw him last? Does anyone know?
Don't go near the mud! But I must go!
Keep well away from the rushes! But how?
Has anyone seen my brother? Not for a week now –
he's been eaten
for certain!

And then, one day, it was June, they all saw him.
He was coming slowly up out of the mud,
they stopped swimming. No one dared
approach, attack. They kept back.

Up a tall reed they saw him climbing
higher and higher, until
he broke the surface, climbing still.

There he stopped, in the wind and the setting sun.
We're safe at last! they cried. *He's gone*!
What became of the monster, was he ill, was he sad?
Was nobody sorry? Had he crept off to die? Was he mad?

Not one of them saw how, suddenly,
as if an invisible knife had touched his back,
he has split, split completely –
his head split like a lid!
The cage is open. Slowly he comes through,
an emperor, with great eyes burning blue.

He rests there, veils of silver a cloak for him.
Night and the little stars travel the black pond,
and now, first light of the day,
his shining cloak wide wings, a flash, a whirr,
a jewelled helicopter,
he's away!

O fully he had served his time,
shunned and unlovely in the drab slime,
for freedom at the end – for the sky –
dazzling hunter, Dragonfly!

Libby Houston

Was Worm

Was worm

swaddled in white
Now tiny queen
in sequin coat
peacockbright

drinks the wind
and feeds
on sweat of the leaves

Is little chinks
of mosaic floating
a scatter
of colored beads

Alighting pokes
with her new black wire
the saffron yokes

On silent hinges
openfolds her wings'
applauding hands
Weaned

from coddling white
to lakedeep air
to blue and green

Is queen

May Swenson

Caterpillar

Brown and furry
Caterpillar in a hurry,
Take your walk
To the shady leaf, or stalk,
Or what not,
Which may be the chosen spot.
No toad spy you,
Hovering bird of prey pass by you;
Spin and die,
To live again a butterfly.

Christina Rossetti

Flying Crooked

The butterfly, a cabbage-white,
(His honest idiocy of flight)
Will never now, it is too late,
Master the art of flying straight,
Yet has – who knows so well as I? –
A just sense of how not to fly:
He lurches here and here by guess
And God and hope and hopelessness.
Even the aerobatic swift
Has not his flying-crooked gift.

Robert Graves

Rook

Old black rook straggling homewards,
Half an hour behind his brothers;
Couldn't-care-less, tattered wreck;
Tail-end-Charlie; flap-rag-rogue;
Blindly glides towards the rookery;
Scorns the farmer and his gun.

Weaving down the dusk-dance flight path,
Scavenge-drunk from tips and cow-pats,
Squabbles in the dark-wood alleys,
Rousing all the roosting rabble;
Mocks the night-watch owl's white passing;
Sleeps in stupor, chuckling darkly.

Keith Wilkins

The Blackbird by Belfast Lough

What little throat
Has framed that note?
What gold beak shot
   It far away?
A blackbird on
His leafy throne
Tossed it alone
   Across the bay.

Anon, about AD 800
(translated from Irish
by Frank O'Connor)

Saint Francis and the Birds

When Francis preached love to the birds
They listened, fluttered, throttled up
Into the blue like a flock of words

Released for fun from his holy lips.
Then wheeled back, whirred about his head,
Pirouetted on brothers' capes,

Danced on the wing, for sheer joy played
And sang, like images took flight.
Which was the best poem Francis made,

His argument true, his tone light.

Seamus Heaney

47

God's Praises

Only a fool would fail
To praise God in his might
When the tiny mindless birds
Praise Him in their flight.

Anon, AD 800
(translated from Irish
by Brendan Kennelly)

48

A Narrow Fellow

A narrow Fellow in the Grass
Occasionally rides –
You may have met Him – did you not
His notice sudden is –

The Grass divides as with a Comb –
A spotted shaft is seen –
And then it closes at your feet
And opens further on –

He likes a Boggy Acre
A Floor too cool for Corn –
Yet when a Boy, and Barefoot –
I more than once at Noon

Have passed, I thought, a Whiplash
Unbraiding in the Sun
When stooping to secure it
It wrinkled, and was gone –

Several of Nature's People
I know, and they know me –
I feel for them a transport
Of cordiality –

But never met this Fellow
Attended, or alone
Without a tighter breathing
And Zero at the Bone –

Emily Dickinson

Father and I in the Woods

'Son,'
My father used to say,
  'Don't run.'

'Walk,'
My father used to say,
  'Don't talk.'

'Words,'
My father used to say,
  'Scare birds.'

So be:
It's sky and brook and bird
  And tree.

David McCord

My Mother
Saw a Dancing Bear

My mother saw a dancing bear
By the schoolyard, a day in June.
The keeper stood with chain and bar
And whistle-pipe, and played a tune.

And bruin lifted up its head
And lifted up its dusty feet,
And all the children laughed to see
It caper in the summer heat.

They watched as for the Queen it died.
They watched it march. They watched it halt.
They heard the keeper as he cried,
'Now, roly-poly!' 'Somersault!'

And then, my mother said, there came
The keeper with a begging-cup,
The bear with burning coat of fur,
Shaming the laughter to a stop.

They paid a penny for the dance,
But what they saw was not the show;
Only, in bruin's aching eyes,
Far-distant forests, and the snow.

Charles Causley

The Caged Bird in Springtime

What can it be,
This curious anxiety?
It is as if I wanted
To fly away from here.

But how absurd!
I have never flown in my life,
And I do not know
What flying means, though I have heard,
Of course, something about it.

Why do I peck the wires of this little cage?
It is the only nest I have ever known.
But I want to build my own,
High in the secret branches of the air.

I cannot quite remember how
It is done, but I know
That what I want to do
Cannot be done here.

I have all I need –
Seed and water, air and light.
Why then, do I weep with anguish,
And beat my head and my wings
Against those sharp wires, while the children
Smile at each other, saying: 'Hark how he sings'?

James Kirkup

The Snare

I hear a sudden cry of pain!
There is a rabbit in a snare:
Now I hear the cry again,
But I cannot tell from where.

But I cannot tell from where
He is calling out for aid!
Crying on the frightened air,
Making everything afraid!

Making everything afraid!
Wrinkling up his little face!
As he cries again for aid:
– And I cannot find the place!

And I cannot find the place
Where his paw is in the snare!
Little One! Oh, Little One!
I am searching everywhere!

James Stephens

Hi!

Hi! handsome hunting man
Fire your little gun.
Bang! Now the animal
Is dead and dumb and done.
Nevermore to peep again, creep again, leap again,
Eat or sleep or drink again, Oh, what fun!

Walter de la Mare

Stop!

Stop! don't swat the fly
Who wrings his hands,
Who wrings his feet.

Kobayashi Issa (1763–1827)
(trans. Geoffrey Bownas and Anthony Thwaite)

Spider

I'm told that the spider
Has coiled up inside her
Enough silky material
To spin an aerial
One-way track
To the moon and back;
Whilst I
Cannot even catch a fly.

Frank Collymore

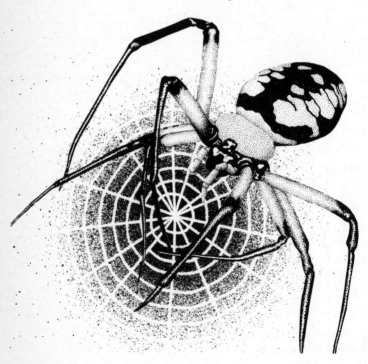

A Poison Tree

I was angry with my friend:
I told my wrath, my wrath did end.
I was angry with my foe:
I told it not, my wrath did grow.

And I water'd it in fears,
Night and morning with my tears;
And I sunned it with smiles,
And with soft deceitful wiles.

And it grew both day and night,
Till it bore an apple bright;
And my foe beheld it shine,
And he knew that it was mine,

And into my garden stole
When the night had veil'd the pole:
In the morning glad I see
My foe outstretch'd beneath the tree.

William Blake (1757–1827)

Survival Kit

'To Dad, for your long journeys.'

Tobacco tin so full it wouldn't rattle.

A nail, diagonal, skewering three figs
already staining the paper scroll
marked 'Contents and Instructions'
in pen-sucked capitals.

Six matches, subdued by candle-wax.

A silver button for flashing coded signals,
dazzling leopards that come too close.

Grandma's hairnet for trapping fish,
mice swept up by whirlwinds,
juicy butterflies.

Chewing-gum for leaks,
'A food that lasts forever'.

Sketches showed where north is,
how to bake an elk in mud,
construct an engine for a floating sleigh.

And in a corner, round three apple-pips,
a coil of string
frayed wildly
as if my son, left-handed,
couldn't use the kitchen scissors,

or had sawn it with the 'knife',
– a sliver of green glass –
its edge darkened
with a quarter-moon of blood.

John Latham

The New House

Now first, as I shut the door,
  I was alone
In the new house; and the wind
  Began to moan.

Old at once was the house,
    And I was old;
My ears were teased with the dread
    Of what was foretold,

Nights of storm, days of mist, without end;
    Sad days when the sun
Shone in vain: old griefs and griefs
    Not yet begun.

All was foretold me; naught
    Could I foresee;
But I learned how the wind would sound
    After these things should be.

Edward Thomas

The Door

Go and open the door.
    Maybe outside there's
    a tree, or a wood,
    a garden,
    or a magic city.

Go and open the door.
  Maybe a dog's rummaging.
  Maybe you'll see a face,
or an eye,
or the picture
  of a picture.

Go and open the door.
  If there's a fog
  it will clear.

Go and open the door.
  Even if there's only
  the darkness ticking,
even if there's only
  the hollow wind,
  even if
          nothing
                  is there,
  go and open the door.

At least
there'll be
a draught.

Miroslav Holub
(trans. Ian Milner and George Theiner)

Books

Believe the golden stories in your head
And all the golden stories that you read,
For what you deeply feel
As true is much more real
Than all that can be counted, cold and dead.

John Kitching

The North Ship:
Legend

I saw three ships go sailing by,
Over the sea, the lifting sea,
And the wind rose in the morning sky,
And one was rigged for a long journey.

The first ship turned towards the west,
Over the sea, the running sea,
And by the wind was all possessed
And carried to a rich country.

The second turned towards the east,
Over the sea, the quaking sea,
And the wind hunted it like a beast
To anchor in captivity.

The third ship drove towards the north,
Over the sea, the darkening sea,
But no breath of wind came forth,
And the decks shone frostily.

The northern sky rose high and black
Over the proud unfruitful sea,
East and west the ships came back
Happily or unhappily:

But the third went wide and far
Into an unforgiving sea
Under a fire-spilling star,
And it was rigged for a long journey.

Philip Larkin

This is the Key
of the Kingdom

This is the key of the kingdom:
In that kingdom there is a city.
In that city there is a town.
In that town there is a street.
In that street there is a lane.
In that lane there is a yard.
In that yard there is a house.
In that house there is a room.
In that room there is a bed.
On that bed there is a basket.
In that basket there are some flowers.
Flowers in a basket.
Basket on the bed.
Bed in the room.
Room in the house.
House in the yard.
Yard in the lane.
Lane in the street.
Street in the town.
Town in the city.
City in the kingdom.
Of that kingdom this is the key.

Traditional

Ages of Man

At ten a child; at twenty wild;
At thirty tame if ever;
At forty wise, at fifty rich;
At sixty good, or never.

Traditional

Riches

My father died a month ago
   And left me all his riches;
A feather bed, a wooden leg,
   And a pair of leather breeches;
A coffee pot without a spout,
   A cup without a handle,
A tobacco pipe without a lid,
   And half a farthing candle.

Traditional

Aunt Julia

Aunt Julia spoke Gaelic
very loud and very fast.
I could not answer her –
I could not understand her.

She wore men's boots
when she wore any.
– I can see her strong foot,
stained with peat,
paddling the treadle of the spinning wheel
while her right hand drew yarn
marvellously out of the air.

Hers was the only house
where I lay at night
in the absolute darkness
of the box bed, listening to
crickets being friendly.

She was buckets
and water flouncing into them.
She was winds pouring wetly
round house-ends.
She was brown eggs, black skirts
and a keeper of threepennybits
in a teapot.

Aunt Julia spoke Gaelic
very loud and very fast.
By the time I had learned
a little, she lay
silenced in the absolute black
of a sandy grave
at Luskentyre.
But I hear her still, welcoming me
with a seagull's voice
across a hundred yards
of peatscapes and lazybeds
and getting angry, getting angry
with so many questions
unanswered.

Norman MacCaig

A Moment of Respect

Two things I remember about my grandfather:
his threadbare trousers, and the way he adjusted
his half-hunter watch two minutes every day.

When I asked him why he needed to know the time so
exactly, he said a business man could lose a fortune
by being two minutes late for an appointment.

When he died he left two meerschaum pipes
and a golden sovereign on a chain. Somebody
threw the meerschaum pipes away, and
there was an argument about the sovereign.

On the day of his burial the church clock chimed
as he was lowered down into the clay, and all
the family advanced their watches by two minutes.

Edwin Brock

529 1983

Absentmindedly,
sometimes,
I lift the receiver
And dial my own number.

(What revelations,
I think then,
If only
I could get through to myself.)

Gerda Mayer

Who are You?

I'm Nobody! Who are you?
Are you – Nobody – too?
Then there's a pair of us?
Don't tell! they'd advertise – you know!

How dreary – to be – Somebody!
How public – like a Frog –
To tell one's name – the livelong June –
To an admiring Bog!

Emily Dickinson

Sally

She was a dog-rose kind of girl:
elusive, scattery as petals;
scratchy sometimes, tripping you like briars.
She teased the boys
twisting this way and that, not to be tamed
or taught any more than the wind.
Even in school the word 'ought'
had no meaning for Sally.
On dull days
she'd sit quiet as a mole at her desk
delving in thought.

But when the sun called
she was gone, running the blue day down
till the warm hedgerows prickled the dusk
and moths flickered out.

Her mother scolded; Dad
gave her the hazel-switch,
said her head was stuffed with feathers
and a starling tongue.
But they couldn't take the shine out of her.
Even when it rained
you felt the sun saved under her skin.
She'd a way of escape
laughing at you from the bright end of a tunnel,
leaving you in the dark.

Phoebe Hesketh

Oath of Friendship

Shang ya!

I want to be your friend
For ever and ever without break or decay.
When the hills are all flat
And the rivers are all dry,
When it lightens and thunders in winter,
When it rains and snows in summer,
When Heaven and Earth mingle –
Not till then will I part from you.

Anon, Chinese, 1st century BC
(trans. Arthur Waley)

Farm Child

Look at this village boy, his head is stuffed
With all the nests he knows, his pockets with flowers,
Snail-shells and bits of glass, the fruit of hours
Spent in the fields by thorn and thistle tuft.
Look at his eyes, see the harebell hiding there;
Mark how the sun has freckled his smooth face
Like a finch's egg under that bush of hair
That dares the wind, and in the mixen now
Notice his poise: from such unconscious grace
Earth breeds and beckons to the stubborn plough.

R. S. Thomas

73

Lazy Man's Song

I could have a job, but am too lazy to choose it;
I have got land, but am too lazy to farm it.
My house leaks; I am too lazy to mend it.
My clothes are torn; I am too lazy to darn them.
I have got wine, but I am too lazy to drink;
So it's just the same as if my cup were empty.
I have got a lute, but am too lazy to play;
So it's just the same as if it had no strings.
My family tells me there is no more steamed rice;
I want to cook, but am too lazy to grind.
My friends and relatives write me long letters;
I should like to read them, but they're such a bother to open.
I have always been told that Hsi Shu-yeh
Passed his whole life in absolute idleness.
But he played his lute and sometimes worked at his forge;
So even *he* was not so lazy as I.

Po Chü-I (772–846)
(trans. Arthur Waley)

Can't be Bothered
To Think of a Title

When they make slouching in the chair
an Olympic sport
I'll be there.

When they give out a cup
for refusing to get up
I'll win it every year.

When they hand out the gold
for sitting by the fire
I'll leave the others in the cold.

And when I'm asked to sign my name
in the Apathetic Hall of Fame
I won't go.

Ian McMillan

75

Catching up on Sleep

i go to bed early
to catch up on my sleep
      but my sleep
is a slippery customer
it bobs and weaves
      and leaves
me exhausted. It
side steps my clumsy tackles
with ease. Bed
raggled I drag
myself to my knees.

The sheep are countless
I pretend to snore
yearn for chloroform
or a sock on the jaw
body sweats heart beats

there is Panic in the Sheets
until
as dawn slopes up the stairs
to set me free
unawares
sleep catches up on me

Roger McGough

The Sloth

In moving-slow he has no Peer.
You ask him something in his ear;
He thinks about it for a Year;

And, then, before he says a Word
There, upside down (unlike a Bird)
He will assume that you have Heard –

A most Ex-as-per-at-ing Lug.
But should you call his manner Smug,
He'll sigh and give his Branch a Hug;

Then off again to Sleep he goes,
Still swaying gently by his Toes,
And you just *know* he knows he knows.

Theodore Roethke

The Vulture

The Vulture eats between his meals
    And that's the reason why
He very, very rarely feels
    As well as you and I.

His eye is dull, his head is bald,
    His neck is growing thinner.
Oh! what a lesson for us all
    To only eat at dinner!

                    Hilaire Belloc

The Considerate Crocodile

There was once a considerate crocodile
Who lay on the banks of the river Nile
And he swallowed a fish with a face of woe,
While his tears ran fast to the stream below.
'I am mourning,' said he, 'the untimely fate
Of the dear little fish that I just now ate!'

Amos R. Wells

The Purist

I give you now Professor Twist,
A conscientious scientist.
Trustees exclaimed, 'He never bungles!'
And sent him off to distant jungles.
Camped on a tropic riverside,
One day he missed his loving bride.
She had, the guide informed him later,
Been eaten by an alligator.
Professor Twist could not but smile.
'You mean,' he said, 'a crocodile.'

Ogden Nash

The Tod's Hole

Now be ye lords or commoners
  Ye needna laugh nor sneer,
For ye'll be a' i' the tod's hole
  In less than a hunner year.

Traditional

(tod = fox)

EPITAPHS

On Charles II

Here lies a Great and Mighty King,
  Whose Promise none rely'd on,
He never said a Foolish thing
  Nor ever did a Wise one.

John Wilmot, Earl of Rochester (1648–80)

On Leslie Moore

Here lies what's left
Of Leslie Moore.
No Les
No more.

Anon

Take Thought

God by land and sea defend you,
Sailors all, who pass my grave;
Safe from wreck his mercy send you –
I am one he did not save.

Plato, about 427–348 BC
(trans. T. F. Higham)

On a Dentist

Stranger, approach this spot with gravity;
John Brown is filling his last cavity.

Anon

Midland Epitaph

'Er as was 'as gone from me.
Us as is'll go ter she.

Anon

Requiem

Under the wide and starry sky,
Dig the grave and let me lie.
Glad did I live and gladly die,
    And I laid me down with a will.

This be the verse you grave for me:
Here he lies where he longed to be;
Home is the sailor, home from sea,
    And the hunter home from the hill.

Robert Louis Stevenson

In This Short Life

In this short Life
That only lasts an hour
How much – how little – is
Within our power

Emily Dickinson

RIDDLES

I was Round and Small like a Pearl

I was round and small like a pearl,
Then long and slender, as brave as an earl.
Since like a hermit I lived in a cell,
And now like a rogue in the wide world I dwell.

Answer: butterfly   *Traditional*

Voiceless it Cries

Voiceless it cries,
Wingless flutters,
Toothless bites,
Mouthless mutters.

Answer: wind   *J. R. R. Tolkien*

What is it More Eyes Doth Wear

What is it more eyes doth wear
     Than forty men within the land,
Which glister as the crystal clear
     Against the sun, when they do stand?

Answer: a peacock's tail   *Traditional*

Hints on Pronunciation
for Foreigners

I take it you already know
Of tough and bough and cough and dough?
Others may stumble but not you,
On hiccough, thorough, lough and through?
Well done! And now you wish, perhaps,
To learn of less familiar traps?

Beware of heard, a dreadful word
That looks like beard and sounds like bird,
And dead: it's said like bed, not bead –
For goodness sake don't call it 'deed'!
Watch out for meat and great and threat
(They rhyme with suite and straight and debt.)

A moth is not a moth in mother
Nor both in bother, broth in brother,
And here is not a match for there
Nor dear and fear for bear and pear,
And then there's dose and rose and lose –
Just look them up – and goose and choose,
And cork and work and card and ward,
And font and front and word and sword,
And do and go and thwart and cart –
Come, come, I've hardly made a start!
A dreadful language? Man alive!
I'd mastered it when I was five!

T. S. W.

Shallow Poem

I've thought of a poem.
I carry it carefully,
nervously, in my head,
like a saucer of milk;
in case I should spill some lines
before I can put it down.

Gerda Mayer

The Scribe's Cat

I and Pangur Bán, my cat,
'Tis a like task we are at:
Hunting mice is his delight,
Hunting words I sit all night . . .

Anon, about AD 800
(translated from Irish by Robin Flower)

The Mouse that Gnawed the Oak-tree Down

The mouse that gnawed the oak-tree down
Began his task in early life.
He kept so busy with his teeth
He had no time to take a wife.

He gnawed and gnawed through sun and rain
When the ambitious fit was on,
Then rested in the sawdust till
A month of idleness had gone.

He did not move about to hunt
The coteries of mousie-men.
He was a snail-paced, stupid thing
Until he cared to gnaw again.

The mouse that gnawed the oak-tree down,
When that tough foe was at his feet –
Found in the stump no angel-cake
Nor buttered bread, nor cheese nor meat –

The forest-roof let in the sky.
'This light is worth the work,' said he.
'I'll make this ancient swamp more light,'
And started on another tree.

Vachel Lindsay

The First Tooth

Through the house what busy joy,
Just because the infant boy
Has a tiny tooth to show!
I have got a double row,
All as white, and all as small;
Yet no one cares for mine at all.
He can say but half a word,
Yet that single sound's preferred
To all the words that I can say
In the longest summer day.
He cannot walk, yet if he put
With mimic motion out his foot,
As if he thought he were advancing,
It's prizèd more than my best dancing.

Charles and Mary Lamb
(1775–1834 and 1764–1847)

Dear Sir

Dear Sir, I'm sorry about my misbehaviour,
So that's why I'm writing this letter,
I'm sorry about your broken leg,
I hope it's getting better.

I'm sorry about the poison ivy,
I'm sorry about the snake,
I'm sorry I didn't realize,
That your life was at stake.

I'm sorry about the itching powder,
That I put down your back,
I honestly didn't mean,
To get you the sack.

I'm sorry about the curry powder,
That I put in your tea,
I'm sorry about the pin on your seat,
I'm glad you didn't see me.

I'm sorry I made you break your table,
I know you went crazy when you got the bill,
I actually didn't mean . . . (I'm sorry),
To make you very ill.

I'm sorry about the bar of soap,
That I set outside the door,
The jokes have gone a little too far,
I promise there won't be any more.

So ends this letter of apology,
I hope you will accept,
I always thought you were a clever guy,
Who would have looked before you leapt!

Stephen Dow (aged 11)

91

School Champion

Learn he could not; he said he could not learn,
But he professed it gave him no concern:
Books were his horror, dinner his delight,
And his amusement to shake hands and fight;
Argue he could not, but in case of doubt,
Or disputation, fairly boxed it out:
This was his logic, and his arm so strong,
His cause prevailed, and he was never wrong.

George Crabbe (1754–1832)

Speak Roughly to Your Little Boy

Speak roughly to your little boy,
   And beat him when he sneezes:
He only does it to annoy,
   Because he knows it teases.

    Chorus
   Wow! wow! wow!

I speak severely to my boy,
   I beat him when he sneezes;
For he can thoroughly enjoy
   The pepper when he pleases!

    Chorus
   Wow! wow! wow!

    Lewis Carroll (1832–98)

Demeanour

Busy in study be thou, child,
And in the hall, meek and mild,
And at the table, merry and glad,
And at bed, soft and sad.

Anon (16th century)

The Parent

Children aren't happy with nothing to ignore,
And that's what parents were created for.

Ogden Nash

The Hag

The Hag is astride,
  This night for to ride;
The Devil and she together:
  Through thick and through thin,
  Now out and then in,
Though ne'er so foul be the weather.

A thorn or a burr
  She takes for a spur:
With a lash of a bramble she rides now,
  Through brakes and through briars,
  O'er ditches and mires,
She follows the Spirit that guides now.

No Beast for his food,
  Dares now range the wood;
But hushed in his lair he lies lurking:
  While mischiefs, by these,
  On land and on seas,
At noon of night are a-working.

The storm will arise
  And trouble the skies;
This night, and more for the wonder,
  The ghost from the tomb
  Affrighted shall come,
Called out by the clap of the thunder.

Robert Herrick (1591–1674)

There Came a Day

There came a day that caught the summer
Wrung its neck
Plucked it
And ate it.

Now what shall I do with the trees?
The day said, the day said.
Strip them bare, strip them bare.
Let's see what is really there.

And what shall I do with the sun?
The day said, the day said.
Roll him away till he's cold and small.
He'll come back rested if he comes back at all.

And what shall I do with the birds?
The day said, the day said.
The birds I've frightened, let them flit,
I'll hand out pork for the brave tomtit.

And what shall I do with the seed?
The day said, the day said.
Bury it deep, see what it's worth.
See if it can stand the earth.

What shall I do with the people?
The day said, the day said.
Stuff them with apple and blackberry pie –
They'll love me then till the day they die.

There came this day and he was autumn.
His mouth was wide
And red as a sunset.
His tail was an icicle.

Ted Hughes

The Lonely Scarecrow

He stands alone in rags and tatters,
His body wet with rain.
It's over now and nothing matters
No need to guard the grain.

His hat, once home to a bird
His pocket a home for a mouse
Now they've gone, no more to be heard,
They don't need him as a house.

The cold wind blows and the harvest is in
And creatures of summer depart.
The scarecrow knows winter's about to begin
And loneliness chills his heart.

Darren Mackintosh (aged 8)

Even before His Majesty

Even before His Majesty,
The scarecrow does not remove
His plaited hat.

Dansui, Japan, 17th century
(trans. R. H. Blyth)

Digging

Today I think
Only with scents, – scents dead leaves yield,
And bracken, and wild carrot's seed,
And the square mustard field;

Odours that rise
When the spade wounds the roots of tree,
Rose, currant, raspberry, or goutweed,
Rhubarb or celery;

The smoke's smell, too,
Flowing from where a bonfire burns
The dead, the waste, the dangerous,
And all to sweetness turns.

It is enough
To smell, to crumble the dark earth,
While the robin sings over again
Sad songs of Autumn mirth.

Edward Thomas

Felling Trees

Stop! I cried to them,
    But the noise of their saws
Cut out my final plea.
    Everything is dying;
Dark sky where the flats will be.

Adrian Youd (aged 13)

Snowcat

The snow is a cat,
padding softly, quietly, on all fours.
It falls with no sound,
it gives no warning of its coming,
but pounces when you least expect it.
Then,
when it has come,
it lies and suns itself,
and disappears on its rounds.

Then back at your door,
a stray cat,
an unwanted cat,
swirling around,
spitting and scratching.
Angry,
but lonely.

Clare Fielden (aged 10)

101

Winter Wise

Walk fast in snow, in frost walk slow,
And still as you go tread on your toe;
When frost and snow are both together,
Sit by the fire, and spare shoe leather.

Traditional

How to Behave in a Thunderstorm

Beware of an oak
It draws the stroke;
Avoid an ash,
It courts the flash;
Creep under the thorn,
It will keep you from harm.

Traditional

The Twelve Months

Snowy, Flowy, Blowy,
Showery, Flowery, Bowery,
Hoppy, Croppy, Droppy,
Breezy, Sneezy, Freezy.

George Ellis (1753–1815)

Death of a Snowman

I was awake all night,
Big as a polar bear,
Strong and firm and white.
The tall black hat I wear
Was draped with ermine fur.
I felt so fit and well
Till the world began to stir
And the morning sun swell.
I was tired, began to yawn;
At noon in the humming sun
I caught a severe warm;
My nose began to run.
My hat grew black and fell,
Was followed by my grey head.
There was no funeral bell,
But by tea-time I was dead.

Vernon Scannell

103

Out in the Dark

Out in the dark over the snow
The fallow fawns invisible go
With the fallow doe;
And the winds blow
Fast as the stars are slow.

Stealthily the dark haunts round
And, when a lamp goes, without sound
At a swifter bound
Than the swiftest hound,
Arrives, and all else is drowned;

And I and star and wind and deer
Are in the dark together, – near,
Yet far, – and fear
Drums on my ear
In that sage company drear.

How weak and little is the light,
All the universe of sight,
Love and delight,
Before the might,
If you love it not, of night.

Edward Thomas

Riddle

White bird, featherless,
Flew from Paradise,
Pitched on the castle wall;
Along came Lord Landless,
Took it up handless,
And rode away horseless
To the King's white hall.

Traditional

Answer: snow and sun

Li Fu-Jên

The sound of her silk skirt has stopped.
On the marble pavement dust grows.
Her empty room is cold and still.
Fallen leaves are piled against the doors.
  Longing for that lovely lady
How can I bring my aching heart to rest?

Wu-ti (157–87 BC)
(trans. Arthur Waley)

The Warm and The Cold

Freezing dusk is closing
  Like a slow trap of steel
On trees and roads and hills and all
  That can no longer feel.
    But the carp is in its depth
      Like a planet in its heaven.
    And the badger in its bedding
      Like a loaf in the oven.
    And the butterfly in its mummy
      Like a viol in its case.
    And the owl in its feathers
      Like a doll in its lace.

Freezing dusk has tightened
  Like a nut screwed tight
On the starry aeroplane
  Of the soaring night.
    But the trout is in its hole
      Like a chuckle in a sleeper.
    The hare strays down the highway
      Like a root going deeper.
    The snail is dry in the outhouse
      Like a seed in a sunflower.
    The owl is pale on the gatepost
      Like a clock on its tower.

Moonlight freezes the shaggy world
    Like a mammoth of ice –
The past and the future
    Are the jaws of a steel vice.
        But the cod is in the tide-rip
            Like a key in a purse.
        The deer are on the bare-blown hill
            Like smiles on a nurse.
        The flies are behind the plaster
            Like the lost score of a jig.
        Sparrows are in the ivy-clump
            Like money in a pig.

Such a frost
    The flimsy moon
        Has lost her wits.

            A star falls.

The sweating farmers
    Turn in their sleep
        Like oxen on spits.

Ted Hughes

The Frozen Man

Out at the edge of town
where black trees

crack their fingers
in the icy wind

and hedges freeze
on their shadows

and the breath of cattle,
still as boulders,

hangs in rags
under the rolling moon,

a man is walking
alone:

on the coal-black road
his cold

feet
ring

and
ring.

Here in a snug house
at the heart of town

the fire is burning
red and yellow and gold:

you can hear the warmth
like a sleeping cat

breathe softly
in every room.

When the frozen man
comes to the door,

let him in,
let him in,
let him in.

Kit Wright

109

Singing in the Streets

I had almost forgotten the singing in the streets,
Snow piled up by the houses, drifting
Underneath the door into the warm room,
Firelight, lamplight, the little lame cat
Dreaming in soft sleep on the hearth, mother dozing,
Waiting for Christmas to come, the boys and me
Trudging over blanket fields waving lanterns to the sky.
I had almost forgotten the smell, the feel of it all,
The coming back home, with girls laughing like stars,
Their cheeks, holly berries, me kissing one,
Silent-tongued, soberly, by the long church wall;
Then back to the kitchen table, supper on the white cloth,
Cheese, bread, the home-made wine:
Symbols of the Night's joy, a holy feast.
And I wonder now, years gone, mother gone,
The boys and girls scattered, drifted away with the
    snowflakes,

Lamplight done, firelight over,
If the sounds of our singing in the streets are still there,
Those old tunes, still praising:
And now, a life-time of Decembers away from it all,
A branch of remembering holly spears my cheeks,
And I think it may be so;
Yes, I believe it may be so.

Leonard Clark

When Icicles Hang by the Wall

When icicles hang by the wall,
   And Dick the shepherd blows his nail,
And Tom bears logs into the hall,
   And milk comes frozen home in pail;
When blood is nipped, and ways be foul,
Then nightly sings the staring owl.
Tu-whit, tu-who! a merry note,
While greasy Joan doth keel the pot.

When all aloud the wind doth blow,
    And coughing drowns the parson's saw,
And birds sit brooding in the snow,
    And Marian's nose looks red and raw,
When roasted crabs hiss in the bowl,
Then nightly sings the staring owl,
Tu-whit, tu-who! a merry note,
While greasy Joan doth keel the pot.

William Shakespeare

Reindeer Report

Chimneys: colder.
Flightpaths: busier.
Driver: Christmas (F)
Still baffled by postcodes.

Children: more
And stay up later.
Presents: heavier.
Pay: frozen.

Mission in spite
Of all this
Accomplished:

MERRY CHRISTMAS

U. A. Fanthorpe

What the Donkey Saw

No room in the inn, of course,
And not that much in the stable,
What with the shepherds, Magi, Mary,
Joseph, the heavenly host –
Not to mention the baby
Using our manger as a cot.
You couldn't have squeezed another cherub in
For love or money.

Still, in spite of the overcrowding,
I did my best to make them feel wanted.
I could see the baby and I
Would be going places together.

U.A. Fanthorpe

Carol

Mary laid her Child among
  The bracken-fronds of night –
And by the glimmer round His head
  All the barn was lit.

Mary held her Child above
  The miry, frozen farm –
And by the fire within His limbs
  The resting roots were warm.

Mary hid her Child between
  Hillocks of hard sand –
By singing water in His veins
  Grass sprang from the ground.

Mary nursed her Child beside
  The gardens of a grave –
And by the death within His bones
  The dead became alive.

Norman Nicholson

Thaw

Over the land freckled with snow half-thawed
The speculating rooks at their nests cawed
And saw from elm-tops, delicate as flower of grass,
What we below could not see, Winter pass.

Edward Thomas

Dear March –

Dear March – Come in –
How glad I am –
I hoped for you before –
Put down your Hat –
You must have walked –
How out of Breath you are –
Dear March, how are you, and the Rest –
Did you leave Nature well –
Oh March, Come right up stairs with me –
I have so much to tell –

I got your Letter, and the Birds –
The Maples never knew that you were coming – till I called
I declare – how Red their Faces grew –
But March, forgive me – and
All those Hills you left for me to Hue –
There was no Purple suitable –
You took it all with you –

Who knocks? That April.
Lock the Door –
I will not be pursued –
He stayed away a Year to call
When I am occupied –
But trifles look so trivial
As soon as you have come

That Blame is just as dear as Praise
And Praise as mere as Blame –

Emily Dickinson

For, Lo, the Winter is Past

For, lo, the winter is past
The rain is over and gone;
The flowers appear on the earth;
The time of the singing of birds is come
And the voice of the turtle is
    heard in our land.

from *The Song of Solomon*, The Old Testament

Acknowledgements

Special thanks are due to my editor, Phyllis Hunt, for her never-failing patience and efficiency in the face of innumerable inquiries, and to my long-suffering librarian Elaine Thielen – who also kept smiling!

The editor gratefully acknowledges permission to use the following copyright material:

Extracts from the Authorized King James version of the Bible, which is Crown Copyright in the United Kingdom, are reproduced by permission of Eyre and Spottiswoode (Publishers) Ltd, Her Majesty's Printers, London.

Brock, Edwin 'A Moment of Respect' from *Penguin Modern Poets 8*, by permission of the author and Penguin Books Ltd.

Carey, Leo 'Water' reprinted by permission of the author.

Causley, Charles 'Miller's End', 'Tell Me, Tell Me, Sarah Jane' and 'My Mother Saw a Dancing Bear' from *Figgie Hobbin* by permission of the author and Macmillan.

Clark, Leonard 'Singing in the Streets' reprinted by permission of Robert A. Clark, Literary Executor of Leonard Clark.

Davide, Adèle 'I Know Things' reprinted by permission of the author.

De La Mare, Walter 'Hi!' by permission of The Literary Trustees of Walter de la Mare and The Society of Authors as their representative.

Dickinson, Emily 'A Narrow Fellow', 'I'm Nobody!', 'To Make a Prairie', 'In This Short Life' and 'Dear March' reprinted by permission of the publishers and the Trustees of Amherst

College from *The Poems of Emily Dickinson*, edited by Thomas H. Johnson, Cambridge, Mass: The Belknap Press of Harvard University Press, Copyright 1951, © 1955, 1979, 1983 by The President and Fellows of Harvard College.

Dow, Stephen 'Dear Sir' from *Cadbury's Third Book of Children's Poetry* published by Beaver Books, copyright © Cadbury Ltd. 1985, reprinted by permission of Cadbury Ltd. and of the author.

Fanthorpe, U.A. 'Reindeer Report' and 'What the Donkey Saw' first published in *Poems for Christmas* (Peterloo Poets, 1981). Reprinted by permission of the author and of Harry Chambers, Peterloo Poets.

Farjeon, Eleanor 'Waves of the Sea' from *The Children's Bells* published by Oxford University Press. (Reprinted by permission of David Higham Associates Ltd.)

Fielden, Clare 'Snowcat' reprinted by permission of the author.

Flower, Robin (trans.) Extract from *Pangur Bán* reprinted by permission of Pat Flower.

Gowar, Mick 'The Painter' from *So Far So Good* by Mick Gowar, published by Collins.

Graves, Robert 'Flying Crooked' from *Collected Poems* (1975), reprinted by permission of A.P. Watt Ltd. on behalf of the Executors of the Estate of Robert Graves.

Heaney, Seamus 'St Francis and the Birds' from *Death of a Naturalist* by Seamus Heaney, published by Faber and Faber Ltd. Reprinted by permission of Faber and Faber Ltd.

Hesketh, Phoebe 'Sally' from *Song of Sunlight*, reprinted by permission of The Bodley Head.

Hoberman, Mary Ann 'Yellow Butter Purple Jelly Red Jam Black Bread' from *Yellow Butter Purple Jelly Red Jam Black Bread* by Mary Ann Hoberman. Copyright © 1981 by Mary Ann

Hoberman. Reprinted by permission of Viking Penguin Inc.

Holub, Miroslav 'The Door' from Miroslav Holub: *Selected Poems* trans. by Ian Milner and George Theiner (Penguin Modern European Poets, 1967) copyright © Miroslav Holub, 1967, trans. copyright © Penguin Books Ltd., 1967. Reproduced by permission of Penguin Books Ltd.

Houston, Libby 'Dragonfly' from *At the Mercy* by Libby Houston, pub. Allison and Busby, reprinted by permission of the author.

Hughes, Ted 'There Came a Day' and 'The Warm and The Cold' from *Season Songs* by Ted Hughes (Faber and Faber). Reprinted by permission of Faber and Faber Ltd.

Issa, Kobayashi 'Stop! Don't swat the fly' by Kobayashi Issa from *The Penguin Book of Japanese Verse* trans. by Geoffrey Bownas and Anthony Thwaite (Penguin Poets, 1964), copyright © Geoffrey Bownas and Anthony Thwaite, 1964. Reproduced by permission of Penguin Books Ltd.

Kennedy, X. J. 'Bee' from *Did Adam Name the Vinegarroon* by X.J. Kennedy. Copyright © 1982 by X.J. Kennedy. Reprinted by permission of David R. Godine, Publisher, Inc.

Kennelly, Brendan 'The Viking Terror' and 'God's Praises' trans. by Brendan Kennelly, 'Blackbird by Belfast Lough' trans. by Frank O'Connor from the *Penguin Book of Irish Verse*, reprinted by permission of Brendan Kennelly.

Kitching, John 'Books' reprinted by permission of the author.

Kirkup, James 'Caged Bird in Springtime' from *A Children's Zoo* comp. by Julia Watson (Fontana Lions), reprinted by permission of Collins.

Latham, John 'Survival Kit' reprinted by permission of the author.

Larkin, Philip 'The North Ship: Legend' from *The North Ship* by Philip Larkin (Faber and Faber). Reprinted by permission of Faber and Faber Ltd.

MacCaig, Norman 'Aunt Julia' from *The Collected Poems of Norman MacCaig*. Reprinted by permission of the author and Chatto and Windus The Hogarth Press.

Mackintosh, Darren 'The Lonely Scarecrow' first appeared in *Junior Education*, December 1986, and is reprinted by permission of the author.

Mayer, Gerda 'Shallow Poem' and '529 1983' reprinted by permission of the author.

McCord, David 'Father and I in the Woods' from *Mr Bidery's Spidery Garden*, published by Harrap and reprinted by permission of the publisher. Also from *Far and Few* by David McCord. Copyright 1952 by David McCord. Reprinted by permission of Little, Brown and Co.

McGough, Roger 'What my Lady Did' from *Waving at Trains* and 'Catching up on Sleep' from *In The Glassroom*, both by Roger McGough and published by Jonathan Cape. Reprinted by permission of the author.

McMillan, Ian 'Can't be Bothered to Think of a Title' reprinted by permission of the author.

Millay, Edna St Vincent 'Counting-out rhyme' and 'Low-Tide' by Edna St Vincent Millay from *Collected Poems*, Harper and Row. Copyright © 1921, 1928, 1948, 1955 by Edna St Vincent Millay and Norma Millay Ellis. Reprinted by permission.

Nash, Ogden 'The Purist' and 'The Parent' from *I Wouldn't Have Missed It*, reprinted by permission of André Deutsch.

Nichols, Grace 'Sea Timeless Song' from *The Fat Black Woman's Poems* by Grace Nichols, published by Virago Press, reprinted by permission of Virago Press.

Nicholson, Norman 'Carol' from *Five Rivers* by Norman Nicholson. Reprinted by permission of Faber and Faber Ltd.

Plato 'Take Thought' by Plato, trans. T.F. Higham, from *The Oxford Book of Greek Verse in Translation* ed. by T.F. Higham and C.M. Bowra (1938). Reprinted by permission of Oxford University Press.

Rawling, Tom 'The Names of the Sea-trout' reprinted from *The Old Showfield* (Taxus Press) by permission of the author.

Reeves, James 'Grim and Gloomy' by James Reeves, © James Reeves Estate. Reprinted by permission of The James Reeves Estate.

Roethke, Theodore 'My Papa's Waltz' and 'The Sloth' from *The Collected Poems of Theodore Roethke*, reprinted by permission of Faber and Faber Ltd. 'My Papa's Waltz' copyright 1942 by Hearst Magazines, Inc. and 'The Sloth' copyright 1950 by Theodore Roethke from *The Collected Poems of Theodore Roethke*. Reprinted by permission of Doubleday and Co. Inc.

Scannell, Vernon 'Death of a Snowman' reprinted by permission of the author.

Stephens, James 'The Snare' by permission of The Society of Authors on behalf of the copyright owner, Mrs Iris Wise.

Swenson, May 'Was Worm' by May Swenson is reprinted by permission of the author, copyright © 1958. Renewed 1986 by May Swenson, and first published in the collection *A Cave of Spines*, 1958.

Thomas, R.S. 'Farm Child' from *Song at the Year's Turning* by permission of Grafton Books, a division of the Collins Publishing Group.

Tolkien, J.R.R. Riddle from *The Hobbit* by J.R.R. Tolkien, reprinted by permission of Allen and Unwin.

Updike, John 'Winter Ocean' from *Telegraph Poles* by John Updike, reprinted by permission of André Deutsch Ltd.

Waley, Arthur (trans.) 'Lazy Man's Song', 'Oath of Friendship' and 'Li Fu-Jên' from *Chinese Poems* reprinted by permission of Allen and Unwin.

Wilkins, Keith 'Rook'. Reprinted by permission of the author.

Wright, Kit 'The Frozen Man' from *Rabbiting On* by Kit Wright, reprinted by permission of Collins Publishers.

Youd, Adrian 'Felling Trees' first appeared in a Jersey schools' anthology and is reprinted by permission of the author.

Yoruba Poem 'Leopard' from *Yoruba Poetry* comp. Ulli Beier, pub. Cambridge University Press. Reprinted by permission of Cambridge University Press.

Acknowledgements are also made to the few copyright-holders whom the editor has been unable to trace in spite of careful inquiry.

Index of Poets

125